D1116154

THE GEESE AND THE TORTOISE

AND OTHER STORIES

Retold by: **MRUDUL TATA**
Illustrated by: **HOLLEY BENTON**

TATA PUBLISHING

Copyright © 1995 by Mrudul Tata.

All rights, including the right of presentation or reproduction in whole or in part in any form, are reserved under the Universal Copyright Convention.

This book must not be published in any form without written permission from the Publisher.

First Impression 1995.

Printed in Hong Kong.

Library of Congress Catalog Card Number 94-90320

ISBN 0-9639913-1-0

INTRODUCTION

Long ago there lived an Indian King who had three sons. The princes were very dull and lazy. Many teachers were tried but the princes were unable to learn anything. Then one day a learned old man undertook the task of teaching them. He told them stories of birds and animals which the princes listened to very attentively and from the stories learned the art of living a life where friendship, trust and respect play a very important role. This collection of ancient stories originally written in Sanskrit is known as "The Panchatantra." Some of the most popular of these stories have been retold in this book.

Dedicated to Ganesh, Lord of Wisdom

CONTENTS

THE CROWS AND THE SNAKE

A huge banyan tree stood serenely on the bank of a lovely river. Many beautiful birds made their nests in its branches. Among the birds was a pair of crows who had their simple nest on the lower branches of the tree. The crows had lived on the tree for a very long time and had raised many young ones.

One hot afternoon, a large black snake came creeping out of the jungle and coiled itself in the hollow of the trunk at the foot of the tree. The birds were terrified. They knew he was dangerous, but there was nothing they could do.

It was soon time for the mother crow to lay her eggs. Everyday the crows kept a careful watch over their precious eggs to make sure no harm would come to them. The snake waited patiently, pretending to show no interest in the eggs.

The crows were quite relieved that the snake seemed to pose no threat. One day, they decided it was safe to leave their nest and go in search of food together. As soon as the crows flew off, the snake uncoiled itself and slithered up the tree. In a flash, his jaws opened wide and he gulped down the crows' eggs.

When the crows came back and found their nest empty, they were heartbroken. They went from branch to branch to see if they could find their eggs, but it was to no avail.

Full of sorrow the mother crow sobbed, "My dear husband, we have to leave this tree and go elsewhere. There is no way we can be safe from the snake."

Although he shared the grief of his wife, the father crow was reluctant to leave the tree. He shook his head and replied softly, "No my dearest, we must save our home. Let me seek the advice of my clever old friend, the fox." So the next day, he went to see the fox and told him what had happened.

The fox pondered for a while and said, "Dear friend, listen carefully! Every afternoon the princess comes to the river to swim with her friends. Before they start swimming, they leave all their jewelry on the river bank with the rest of their things. As soon as the princess is in the water, you must pick up her gold necklace. Meanwhile your wife must caw as loudly as she can. You should then fly with the necklace and drop it in the hollow of the tree trunk."

The next day the crows waited for the princess and her friends to arrive at the river. The princess took off her beautiful gold necklace studded with diamonds and rubies, and gently placed it on top of her clothes. When all the ladies started swimming, the father crow swiftly scooped up the gold necklace while the mother crow started cawing loudly. Hearing the noise the servants looked up, and noticing the gold necklace in the crow's beak they chased after him.

Making sure the servants were following them, the crows flew to the banyan tree and dropped the necklace in the hollow of the trunk.

The black snake, with the glittering gold necklace coiled around his head, came out to see what all the din was about. Swaying from side to side, he hissed in anger while flickering his forked tongue and flashing his fangs. Seeing the snake with the necklace, the servants started beating him with their sticks. Full of fear, the snake slinked away to the jungle, never to return.

The crows rejoiced to see the snake flee. The air was filled with the sweet chirping and twittering of young chicks. Once again, the birds on the tree were able to live in peace and harmony.

THE FOUR FRIENDS

Once upon a time a beautiful spotted deer lived in a jungle. Her best friends were a tortoise, a crow and a mouse. Every afternoon the four friends would go to the river together for a drink of water. As the tortoise, crow, and mouse gathered one afternoon at their usual meeting place, the deer did not come.

After waiting patiently for a long time, the tortoise finally said to the crow, "I am afraid that our friend must be in trouble. Why don't you fly around and see if you can find her? Before long dusk will change to night and it will get dark."

So the crow circled high up in the air and started calling out to the deer. Soon he heard a feeble, scared voice crying, "Help me! Help me!" The crow immediately flew down, and to his dismay saw the deer struggling in a net.

"Please save me! I am caught in a hunter's net and I cannot escape," she pleaded to the crow.

"Do not worry," answered the crow, "we will help you escape." He flew back to the tortoise and mouse, and told them what had happened.

The tortoise thought for a while and said to the crow, "If you can give the mouse a ride on your back, he can gnaw at the net with his teeth and free the deer. I will catch up with you and we will all come back together."

The crow flew up in the air with the mouse on his back and the tortoise followed. As soon as the mouse reached the deer, he started working on the net and set his friend free. After a while the tortoise joined them, but just as they were rejoicing they heard the hunter's footsteps. Quickly deciding to hide, the mouse scurried behind a large stone, the crow perched high on a tree, and the deer ran away as far as she could. But the tortoise could not hide. He was very slow and had not gone very far when the hunter approached.

The hunter was surprised to find the net empty. Just as he was wondering what to do, he saw the tortoise lumbering towards a large shrub. Thinking that the tortoise would be equally good for dinner, he caught the tortoise and put him in a sack. As soon as the others saw what had happened, they again got together to find a way to help the tortoise.

The deer said, "My friends, it is my turn to help. I will go and stand in front of the hunter. When he sees me, he will drop the sack and start chasing me."

The crow thought that the plan was too risky. He turned to the deer and said, "But what if the hunter catches you? Please do be careful!"

"Do not worry about me," replied the deer. "I can run as fast as the wind."

So the crow took the mouse on his back and flew high up on a tree. The deer ran quietly through the bushes to wait for the hunter. When she heard footsteps approaching, the deer bounded in full view of the hunter.

As soon as the hunter saw the deer, he dropped the sack and started chasing her. In the meantime, the mouse and the crow opened the sack, and set the tortoise free. Hiding behind dense shrubs, they waited anxiously for the deer to return.

The fleet footed deer swiftly disappeared into the jungle. After chasing her for a long time, the hunter finally gave up. Tired and hungry, he returned to fetch the tortoise, only to find an empty sack.

As the hunter walked home, he saw in the far distance a spotted deer, a crow, a tortoise and a mouse gathered together. Shaking his head in wonder, the hunter knew that the four friends had outwitted him.

THE GEESE AND THE TORTOISE

Once there lived in a pool an old tortoise. He had two young geese for friends. The geese would come to the pool every day to listen to the ancient fables that the tortoise was fond of telling.

The seasons passed and it was time for the monsoon. But the rains did not come. Instead of the cool green of the forest and the sapphire blue waters of the pool, there was the parched brown of drought. Soon there was famine. Birds and animals started dying.

The geese came to seek the advice of their friend the tortoise. "O wise one," they said in despair, "we are doomed. What shall we do?"

The tortoise replied, "Do not give up hope. Far over the horizon, there is a forest lush with greenery and a pool with crystal clear waters. Let us go there."

"We can fly to a different land, but you cannot. How will we find this place without you?" the geese said.

"I know I cannot fly like you," answered the tortoise, "but there is a way I can go with you."

"Pray tell us how!" said the geese.

The tortoise asked the two geese to fetch a sturdy stick. When they found a stick the tortoise said, "If each of you can hold one end of the stick with your bills, I shall hold on to the middle with my mouth and you can take me with you."

The geese thought for a while and said, "There is only one danger in this plan."

"What is it?" asked the tortoise impatiently.

"Well," said the geese, "we can carry you in the air with the help of a stick, but if you open your mouth, you will fall."

"Do not worry about me," said the tortoise curtly. "I will not open my mouth."

So the geese agreed to take the tortoise along with them. They swiftly carried the tortoise across barren hills and desolate valleys. Soon they flew over a small village dotted with mud huts. The poor villagers looked up and were surprised to see the sight of two geese carrying a tortoise. Everybody clapped their hands in wonder and pointed to the sky.

The tortoise was convinced that the people were praying to him. "After all," he thought to himself, "am I not leading my friends to a better land?" He opened his mouth to say some words of wisdom. Just as he did so, he lost hold of the stick and fell down to the ground.

The humble geese flew on over the horizon.